Travels with an Umbrella
an
irish
journey

Travels with an Umbrella

an Irish journey

Louis Gauthier

translated by Linda Leith

NUAGE
EDITIONS

Cover design by Terry Gallagher/Doowah Design.
Photo of Louis Gauthier by Danielle Roger.
Printed and bound in Canada by Veilleux Impression à Demande.

We acknowledge the support of The Canada Council for the
Arts and the Manitoba Arts Council for our publishing program.

Canadian Cataloguing in Publication Data

Gauthier, Louis, 1944–
[Voyage en Irlande avec un parapluie. English]
        Travels with an umbrella : an Irish journey

ISBN 0-921833-68-7

        I. Leith, Linda   II. Title.   III. Title: Voyage en
Irlande avec un parapluie. English.

PS8563.A86V6913 1999   C813'.54   C99-901333-5
PQ3919.2.G38V6913 1999

Nuage Editions, P.O. Box 206, RPO Corydon
Winnipeg, Manitoba, R3M 3S7

"If it's true that inaction is always unbearable, imagine how it must torment a man with wet feet."

—Captain W.E. Johns,
Biggles Sees It Through

It's four o'clock in the afternoon and the bars are closed. Large white clouds are rolling across the blue sky. It's cold. I'm walking through deserted streets looking for a place to leave my gear, a kind of army bag, a soft cylinder in rough cloth with leather handles and a strap. Real army bags are khaki; mine is blue. I bought it just before leaving. As soon as I'd stuffed my sleeping bag into it, it was obvious there was room for practically nothing else.

The village is on a small cliff. To one side a long road slopes down to the wharf. The countryside is wide; you can see far in all directions, over land, over sea. The wind is strong, the weather changing. Behind the white clouds large grey clouds with black bellies are rolling in. Here and there, patches of blue sky, fewer and farther between. Out at sea the small waves are capped with foam. In the village, no one. It feels abandoned. I make my way down to the wharf to check the ferry schedule. Rain begins falling gently, a soft, barely perceptible rain.

The ferry won't be leaving till tomorrow. On the beach, I pass a couple of French tourists, and we chat for a bit, our feet in the sand, sheltered by the arch of a small stone building that must be for the use of bathers, closed now for the season. Then I climb back up the road through rain that's suddenly gotten much heavier. There isn't anything particularly heroic about putting one foot in front of the other, but there's nothing else to do. I'll be drenched, but that's just too bad. Walking allows you to appreciate distances for what they are. You panic a bit at first, and then you calm down. There's no way of going any faster.

All kinds of thoughts cross my mind. What if Jesus were to appear to me now, in the flesh, in flesh and bone? And what if He were just that, flesh and bone, what would I do then? What if He weren't the fellow with the beard and the long hair and the kind face, but a short chubby guy with the look of an insurance salesman? What if a guy like that were to say, 'Come, follow me'? I remember an image from my childhood, a kind of holy picture: here was this Christ with such a long but somehow marvelously sweet face, tragic and appealing, and underneath, in red ink, this sentence: What would Jesus do and say in my place? For weeks on end I would ask myself that question about the most trivial matters.

If He were in my place today, Jesus would be putting one foot in front of the other with water trickling down His neck and licks of wet hair plastered on His forehead. Basically, though, I figure He would never have gotten Himself into such a situation. Jesus; I'm still under the influence of that Jehovah's Witness. But why didn't he invite me to Kingdom Hall? Why didn't he invite me to sleep there like a poor Christian?

There's not another soul on the road, and I can't manage anything more than just to keep on walking, more and more afflicted with a sense that I'm not the hero of any novel, just a poor sod grappling with life and ordinariness. But maybe heroes have moments like this too, moments with nothing grand at all about them, moments when there's nothing for it but to put one foot after the other and climb back up the path of their own despair. The air is good and the rain refreshing, but nothing is happening, nothing is taking its course, and inside my head the countryside is being undermined by words and its glory is being whittled away by an unbearable feeling of emptiness and uselessness.

Five o'clock, now, and the bars are still not open: the pub hours are fairly short here. I'm pissed off with this village, it's too pretty and too unwelcoming, pissed off with these decent, empty stone houses, these organized lives with no room for the unexpected. I want to sit down somewhere warm and have a beer. I don't know what else to do at five in the afternoon, when the day is growing just a bit long, the silence just a bit too much to bear. What else to do at such a time than find a bar and allow memory to take over bit by bit, tell myself my story the way it might be told to posterity—and, when I've had one too many, make up inanities no one will ever know about. I'm alone, I have no desire to talk to anyone, so who is it I can't seem to stop talking to...

→

That was in Fishguard, in the heart of Wales, the day before I boarded the boat to Ireland. The Jehovah's Witness had driven me from Cardigan, further north on the coast. I'd hitched a ride outside the village, on the edge of a road shored up by steep embankments of earth and lined with windblown willows. It was cold, and from time to time the squalls forced me to open my umbrella, which the wind practically ripped out of my hand. The road was deserted; I couldn't find shelter anywhere. There were very few cars, and they drove right past me. I was glad when this one pulled up.

A wet Sunday morning. The kind of day you're better off indoors, in the warm, reading by the stove and smoking your pipe while the children play in a corner. What was I doing on the road?

I tell my story once again—the wish to see the world, the need to make a move, break out of the routine, all pretty vague stuff, plausible enough, just to test the waters. I never give the real reasons right away; only if it looks OK. I have a different version for everyone, customized, specially adapted to the circumstances.

This particular guy irritates me. I don't like his head, his soft-featured round face. He's exactly my age, but he looks ten years older, and he talks in a smug kind of way. Yes, yes, he too has traveled. He and his wife did go that one time to France. Brittany, Normandy, Paris. It really wasn't worth the trouble. There's nowhere more beautiful than this part of the country, lots of tourists have told him so. The sea, the mountains, sun in summer, sometimes a bit of snow in winter, the beach, the countryside, and the city not too far away. The city is Swansea, but Swansea or Paris, they're both cities. There's no use chasing around the world. He quotes the Bible at me, chapter and verse. The Bible says to stay at home—especially if you have the great good luck to live in Fishguard— and tend to the state of your everlasting soul.

I light up a cigarette. He remarks primly that the body is God's temple. He himself doesn't smoke, nor does he drink. I dearly wish I had a mickey of Southern Comfort in my pocket. I don't like being lectured, lectures get my goat. Every time I drink, the lectures I've heard come to mind, clear, precise as a city map, with all their prohibitions, commandments, contradictions. Sure, I'm a lousy Christian. Isn't that why Christ came down to earth? To save sinners?

I check out the countryside, the small signs promising us Fishguard in fifteen miles, ten miles. Eight miles. Sure, I'm interested in religion. And right now, I'm on my way to India. Buddhism, Vedanta, Zen, all that. He looks at me out of the corner of his eye, as if I'm having him on. Buddhism? Poor wretches dying of starvation while their holy cows get worshipped as gods?

We've got to the point of going through a list of various biblical creatures—donkeys, camels, pigs, oxen—and the correct opinion to have of each of them, when we pull into Fishguard. I get out of the car in a sleepy little square. My good Samaritan promptly abandons me; he's on his way to Kingdom Hall to hear the Word of God among his brethren, all of whom are saved, just like him. He might have invited me to join them, but he knows full well I'm unworthy. Just as well. This way I won't end up getting baptized, dunked in some enormous basin of holy water.

$\longrightarrow$

I had left Montreal ten days before. It was raining there, too. It was mid-November, the streets practically empty, the few passersby huddling inside their raincoats with their collars up, black umbrellas held out in front of them, nameless in the night. The three of us were walking through a damp and unpleasant cold that enveloped us like a wet sheet. I don't remember anything special, just that it was the three of us, Angèle, Paul and me. What does it matter? Paul was talking about London, about the English who really were, after all, one of the most civilized peoples on earth, talking about the time he spent in hotels over there, the fabulous sums he'd spent.

Angèle and I weren't connecting much at all. It wasn't the first time. There was practically nothing left between us except for the memory of a passion that was the last thing either of us wanted to risk casting into doubt. So it remained unspoken, as if someone dear to us had died and we had to avoid invoking their memory, even though that very memory was the only thing we had in common. We had changed, both of us, each in our own way, and that put a distance between us and what we had once been.

Angèle seemed preoccupied. We had finally sat down in a restaurant, were drinking red wine, and she was glancing around her.

"How's the writing going?" she asked suddenly.

I told her I wasn't writing any more, didn't want to write any more, was satisfied with nothing but silence. Literature was an illness, I declared, destructive of the organism, dangerous to society, impractical and fundamentally unhealthy.

Angèle laughed at me. Paul said I was writing in secret, that I scribbled away when I got home at night. I laid out my theory of the moment: that life is a fiction in any case. Reality had nothing to do with us. Reality had to do with matter and with spirit, and we were between the two, both the creators of the human fiction and its products. Literature could only end in silence, and you were fooling yourself if you thought otherwise.

Later on, Angèle said she'd like to come along. My heart contracted, and for an instant I felt a great desire to tell her, "Come with me, let's start over again." But that was one of those things that couldn't be said. You don't start over again, not ever. She may have guessed what foolish thought had just crossed my mind. But India didn't interest her. Her dreams were of Italy, Greece, the Mediterranean, gentle countries where life isn't thrown into question on a daily basis but simply accepted as a blessing.

I wanted to go, I wanted to stay. We were OK, no doubt about it, just talking like this without any sense of urgency, eating, drinking; we could have carried on like that, evening after evening. There was something so easy about this life that I had the impression of feeding off the very souls of my friends, lulled by big warm waves of alcohol. Why was it that I'd had enough of all that? What was it that I was lacking? I really couldn't have said.

$\longrightarrow$

The Greyhound bus is plunging into the night, and the problems of Quebec are fading in importance. Gas-station neons against the sky at the end of their steel lampposts, dark fields, black forests. And always, in the smoked glass of the window, the haunting reflection of my own face superimposed on the landscape, its eyes watching me. In the droning comfort of the bus, they are looking for the reason why I'm here, they're monitoring the effects of this peculiar desire of mine to yield to the fates, this wanting not to want. I want to rely on the fates, I've chosen of my free will to rely on the fates, to be right where I am, a prisoner in a bus, whisked away without any safeguards at all, at the mercy of the moods and reflexes of some unknown, normal, neutral bus driver. This is just the way I've wanted it—I've wanted to be staring out the window at an American night that's already giving off different kinds of vibes, like a foreign body; staring out the window at a more anxious night. Or maybe it's the traveler's own consciousness that's giving off these different kinds of vibes. And maybe his consciousness is doing so because it knows all too well what happens when you play this kind of little game, crossing borders and changing codes. And his mind resists. It's right to resist.

→

In the grey November drizzle, a stop about three or four in the morning, a few more hours of fitful sleep, the chalky pallor of the dawn, milky and lukewarm, more and more intricate knots of highway. All of a sudden, just for a few seconds, there's the unreal silhouette of the skyscrapers, then the bus is in the tunnel under the Hudson River, the underground garages of the Port Authority Bus Terminal, and there it stops with a sigh, its motor subsiding.

New York. I don't spend long in New York. I've slept badly, am tired, can't find the information I'm looking for. Aggressive glances, brusque gestures, nothing turns out the way I thought it would, everything gets so complicated, and I tell myself I'd have been better to stay home, wake up gently in a big clean bed with a beautiful cheerful girl and carry on leading my easy everyday life. To make matters worse, it's Thanksgiving Day in New York. The offices of Laker Airlines are closed, the restaurants are crammed because of the parade, the public telephone rejects my Canadian coins, and I'm convinced even the machines have turned against me.

A few hours later, though, things have sorted themselves out; with my ticket in my pocket, I feel alive again. Sitting in a quiet bar, I drink a beer with the studied nonchalance of the seasoned traveler. The only other customer, a blonde in her fifties, interrupts her gossiping with the barman to talk to me. I paint the rosiest picture possible: I'm a writer, I'm leaving this evening for India via England, six months of adventures among gurus, pariahs, maharajahs and elephants festooned with gold and precious stones.

She looks at me with envious eyes: she's always dreamed of writing! I must have heard people tell me that a hundred times; it seems so neat to be a writer when you don't have any idea what it's really like, the pages you rewrite ten times, the lack of money, the discouragement, the thousands of hours of work, the uncertainties, the anonymity, the insecurity, the incomprehension. Not wanting to ruin the effect, though, I content myself with saying that I'm sure she'd be capable of writing if she put her mind to it, and to amuse her I suggest she write a book on countries she's never seen—Nepal, Tibet, Kashmir. I like the sound of these words in this empty bar in Queens, and I hope they'll make her dream.

We exchange a few more pleasantries, then I go on my way, more sure of myself than before. Good luck, take care. She's sure I'll write a great book, and I'm happy to have exchanged a few words today with another human being.

$\longrightarrow$

"Propelled by turbo-reactors, we rip right across the sky, high above clouds, oceans and literatures." I put the cap back on my ballpoint pen, turn over the postcard I bought at the airport to have another look at the gaudy colours of Times Square.

The sun is streaming through the windows, and I feel a deep joy surfacing. Everyone has slept badly, the trolleys from which the stewardesses are serving us breakfast are blocking the narrow aisles, zonked passengers are jostling one another at the door to the toilets, everyone is carrying on their profane activities oblivious of the fact that we're flying high above the earthly world. I take my pen out of my pocket and write Angèle's address on the card.

Pinned against the blue immensity of the sky and the sea, Ireland gleams under the wing of the aircraft, as clear and precise as a relief map. I sip my coffee, unable to take my eyes off the sight. A few white clouds over the sea. The English coast appears and then almost immediately disappears under a blanket of increasingly dense grey fog. Soon the plane begins its descent, a thick cloud obscures the view out the window, and we're thrown into limbo. Then all of a sudden we emerge from the clouds, and the ground appears, many-hued and very close by. An exquisite miniature with herds of beige sheep in a checkerboard of tender green fields, farms tucked away behind hedgerows, each with its pond where large swans are gliding, all this seen from on high.

Heathrow Airport. Customs officers polite as gentlemen. A flawless series of signs carefully guides me to a beautiful olive green train that leaves almost immediately, streaks through red-brick suburbs with a regular and deafening hammering of its wheels on the rails. Victoria Station. I'm euphoric to find myself in the heart of London. I walk, walk for hours, fill my eyes with a thousand marvels, mesmerized by these names I've heard so often, now suddenly real: Piccadilly Circus, Soho Square, Charing Cross, London Bridge, Chelsea, Trafalgar Square, Carnaby Street, the Thames—what a high, I can't get over it, it's like a dream. I've landed in a dream and am wandering about in it at will. And, as in the morning, I feel indescribable gusts of happiness surface in me, great waves of pure joy, tremors of ecstasy and freedom. I owe nobody a thing, nobody knows where I am, what I'm doing, no one knows who I am, it's as though I've turned into nothing, nothing other than this sensitive surface on which the various crossroads of London are imprinting themselves, nothing but a mirror, and all I want is to walk till I drop, drink my fill of this prodigious peace, this prodigious blessedness.

—➤

I'm waiting for Jim in front of the handsome red telephone kiosk you can't miss when you get off the train at Crystal Palace and take the road across from the station. That's where we've arranged to meet. I've never seen him, but he's sure to recognize me from Paul's description.

I check out the cars slowing down, turning or stopping in front of me, smile winningly at complete strangers. They've just come to mail a letter or make a telephone call, haven't a clue why I'm being so friendly. Eventually, a tall guy I hadn't noticed puts his hand on my shoulder.

"I'm Jim!" Tweed jacket, big scarf around his neck, elegant leather boots, he's at least three inches taller than me, and he offers me his hand.

I feel badly dressed, a mess, pathetic.

"Where's your luggage?"

My gear? I left it in London, in a locker. I didn't want to put him out.

→

In the end, it didn't change anything. By the time I've spent two days at his place, I've established my routine: I know where to buy a newspaper, beer, fish 'n chips. The weather is mild and it doesn't rain. Jim's apartment is perfect, modern, on two levels, with a hot shower, colour TV, records, hash, and some good books.

The sky is uniformly grey, but its soft light permeates everything, the grass in the parks, the brown and ruddy corners of the walls.

I stay a week at Jim's place. An easy existence that reminds me more and more of the life I was leading before my departure. Bending an elbow, smoking a joint, schmoozing, laughing, being sociable, here I am again, fattened like a little pig as if there were no way of escaping my destiny, this easy middle-class destiny of having everything function, more or less, at some level; so many ounces of alcohol, so many grams of hash, so many hours of free time, so many cubic meters of comfort.

So the same questions arise. What now?

As soon as I come to a halt, it's as though everything around me stops as well. A kind of thick crust starts to form all over again, everything stagnates and coagulates—and I'm horrified to see that what had for days seemed colourful, bright and lively is suddenly assuming the gloomy contours of routine, of sinking, of despair. London isn't doing it for me any more, I'm right back in the grip of emptiness and uselessness again, oppressed by the same weighty and wearisome questions that spoil everything for me.

Unable to move ahead with my plan to write a spiritualist novel—I seem able only to describe its complex structure, incapable of getting to the heart of it—I figure I haven't set out on a journey just to fall into the same old rut, the habit of ease and oblivion, and I set off for Ireland.

London. The very name London reverberates in my mind now, with its rusts, its golds, the rumbling of its railway trains, the clanking of iron gates shutting, its streets paved with gold, illusions, and Dickensian misery.

$\longrightarrow$

Monday. The ferry leaves Fishguard under a glowering sky. I'm moving from deck to deck, watching the coast fade in the distance. The sea is rough, I'm zigzagging as I walk, holding on, here and there, to the metal railings coated in thick white paint. I've always liked ferries, even between Lévis and Québec, even between Sorel and Berthier. I still have a photo of Angèle on the Tadoussac ferry, her hair whipped by the wind, her shawl draped around her like the tunic of a caryatid, her transparent eyes looking far away as if we were out in the open sea.

Up the stairway, down, from the prow to the poop, I make my way to the upper deck. I'm the only person out here; everyone else is indoors. The rain has started, and I allow myself to be run through by the cold wind, breathing the brisk new air into my lungs. I lean on my elbows on the rear handrail, contemplating the bright wake, the seagulls screaming. I can't get over the romanticism of it all, its opaque and silent mystery. In my giddy state, I feel a perverse temptation to toss my bag into the sea, identification papers, money, return ticket, change of shoes, sweater, shirts, socks, underwear—the whole lot sinking among the indifferent fish, turning around slowly, gently, no longer meaning anything at all, vanished, done with, leaving me there without a name, without a past, just as I am. Identity lost, entire cities engulfed, snatched away in the flux of Time, gulped down, swallowed, annihilated, erased from memory, from memory's bureaucrats, archives, and codes, irredeemably drowned in the blind night of the depths.

I toss the butt of my cigarette as far as I can. It arcs on a current of air for a moment, then ends up among the floating refuse a cook has just thrown overboard. Already the gulls are after that, breaking their flight. One last glance, I head back inside, making my way among the staircases and the doorways with raised sills, and sit down at a table in a kind of large windowed salon at the front of the boat where some of the passengers have settled in.

Throwing his British passport onto the table as if he's taking possession, a tall freak in his thirties dumps his leather bag next to me and lowers himself into the chair beside mine. He looks at me sharply from the bottom of his eyes, without blinking: "Are you motoring?"

"No," I reply. "I'm hitching, just like you." I'm a member of the brotherhood, an ally, a comrade. He gets up without a word, collects his belongings and moves away to another table.

Fine.

I go looking for a beer at the bar while a small blonde with pale eyes, as tiny as a doll, crosses the room, dragging a fat red pack and a mandolin behind her. The boat pitches and rolls violently, you have to calculate every step like a drunk on an unsteady sidewalk. The entire hull of the boat shudders when a wave lifts it up, and then there's a sliding motion. The vibrations of the motor are stronger, the boat skids sideways as it labours to make headway. The stem-post plunges into another wave, the poop lifts and the horizon disappears, reappears, disappears. The two barmen have their hands full, what with glasses and bottles smashing into one another, and I'm worried they'll decide to close the bar. The customers themselves have double the difficulty: they have to keep the beer in the glass for long enough to drink it—and then they have to keep it down.

I've always heard the Irish are serious drinkers: there's one of them, sick, at one table, who vomits on the floor and then lights himself a cigarette and carries on drinking, his two feet in a nauseating puddle. Typical and imbecilic. Holding on to the bar with one hand, I make the acquaintance of a tall red-headed fellow who's heading home after a few months' work in England. I don't understand too much of what he tells me, but that doesn't seem to matter. He buys me a drink and then takes me to visit the hold, where enormous trucks held fast with chains are pulling and pushing with all their might. It reminds me of a cargo of slaves, mechanical version. There's not much else to see, and we go back up by the outer decks.

It's night now, the sky is black and the wind ever stronger. There's not even the faintest star to be seen. I leave the Irish guy struggling with a black grease stain on his fine new pants. In the large salon, everyone has slipped into a kind of bad sleep rocked by the irregular, deafening drone of the engines. Only the tiny blonde is staring at the streaming windows. She really is tiny—tiny hands, tiny fingers, tiny waist, well formed, like a miniature model. She's Scottish and her name is Linda. She comes from a small town near Glasgow, the name of which I didn't catch. I get her to repeat it three times and then give up. Something like Ghgh. I can't think of a single intelligent thing to say to her.

→

The ferry docks just before eleven. It's still windy, but no longer raining. There are some buildings near the wharf, but the village is further off, up the cliff. I set off on foot with Linda. We don't speak.

There are all kinds of silences. Linda's silence is a wall, a battlement erected around her; mine is full of words I can't utter. Linda's silence is a refusal. She has no confidence, she opens no door, there isn't the slightest breach I could try to widen, to pry open. My silence is a wave breaking on this battlement, folding back upon itself, troubled waters, splitting, crashing. I would like to find some way of reaching her, opening her up, taking hold of her, devouring her with love. She's not the least bit interested in being devoured.

In silence, under a perfectly black sky, we scale the night. Down below us is the lighthouse, the ferry still lit up, the dark sea. A dog barks. The village is draped in darkness. Here and there we can make out the heavy bulk of the stone houses, black wooden railings closing off dark courtyards, indistinct buildings with low doorways. The road they've pointed out to us takes us away from the village, veers to the left, climbs a bit higher. We notice the lights of a house. Linda's silence is tinged with relief.

Mrs. Fowley has made tea for the two New Zealanders who got off the same boat we did and who arrived a few minutes before us. There are just enough rooms for everyone. In the small living room full of knick-knacks and souvenirs, we exchange smiles of good will.

Hanish is tall and thin, blond, with a healthy complexion. Christiana has black hair and remarkable dark blue eyes, and the same air of pure, sweet, calm and indestructible happiness. They've come by way of Asia and the Middle East, have seen Hong Kong, the Philippines, India, Pakistan. They travelled through Iran just before the borders were closed, they spent two months in Skopelos, crossed Italy, picked grapes in France. They made it to Wales, where they worked for a while on a farm, looking after horses. They are so kind and their happiness is so impenetrable that you'd think they'd found the key to eternal serenity, that they'll be happy their entire lives, just like that, unthinkingly, that they'll never know the agonies of love and suffering, the tortures and heartbreaks that are the fate of all men and women on this earth. They're going back to New Zealand in six months, after seeing the United States and Hawaii. Each will go back to work. They'll have a family. I feel ill at ease with my torments in the face of this too-perfect couple. I fancy drinking a Scotch or two and talking nonsense.

The little Scotswoman is there too, silent, poised like a porcelain cat at the corner of the coffee table laden with cups and saucers. She listens attentively, pricks her ear in my direction at times, half closes her eyes. For some reason I can think of nothing but inane things to say, asking interview-type questions about Australia, Goa, Tehran. My voice sounds much too deep, monotonous, boring, lacking in conviction. I'm annoyed with myself for not being more fun, and I know I can't do anything about it, not this evening. Everything is set just so in this small living room, it would take a blow from an axe, a terrific scream or shriek to jolt us out of the numb and torpid state we're in.

Linda tells us a bit about life in Ghgh, about how cold it gets indoors in wintertime. They want my opinion. As a Québécois, I represent winter, it's as though I hold copyright on the season. I make a few more inane remarks. Linda talks about Dublin, where she's going to meet up with some friends. I ask her to play something on her mandolin, but she's too tired, it's late. She wants no part of unhappiness, suffering, passion, and I can't wish any of that on her. She's so small, so very small under her enormous red pack, making her way through the emptiness that divides Scotland and Ireland. She's entirely alone on her journey, she has nothing, not a single thing other than her courage, no defence other than her smile, her naïveté, her kindness, and she's so fragile that in order to avoid contact she has to act as though she isn't there at all.

I'm alone this evening in Mrs. Fowley's living room, alone with a couple from New Zealand who allow no one in, alone with a little Scotswoman whose thoughts are somewhere else, alone with my own self, taking myself for someone else, and this other me is tired, too, of being alone.

$\longrightarrow$

She's insane, I'm sure of it.

I happened to meet her at the corner of a street where I was hesitating in the drizzle, not really knowing what direction to head in.

I've spent the day in this wet weather, half-sheltered by my black umbrella, lashed by the seaspray as they used to say in the books I read when I was fourteen years old and dreaming of leaving, of traveling, of being free. This morning was even worse, bitterly cold and pouring rain. The others all left for Dublin right after Mrs. Fowley's abundant breakfast, but I, ambitious tourist that I am, I decided to make a bit of a detour in the south, making the most of the lull. Stopping here and there, at this pub, at that one, I ended up covering the hundred or so kilometers to Cork.

It was in Cork that I was hesitating at the corner of a street, close to a bridge, when I met her by chance. I say by chance, but I'm really the one who went up to her. I could have asked my way of anyone else, but I thought she was pretty, so why not?

Yes, she can tell me where to find a room. The best thing is to head for the Tourist Office. She's going that way herself, will take me there.

She's a queer fish, in a bit of a whirl, a nervous kind of whirl. I come from Montreal? She really likes

Canada, she's lived in Toronto, her whole story spills out at breakneck speed, something about her husband being over there, I don't have time to say anything to halt the flow of words, let her know I understand only part of what she's saying, she isn't even looking my way, is she talking to herself, or what? We're splashing our way through puddles of water and mud that the lorries have trailed into the city from the countryside, I'm reduced to guesswork, and my hunch is her husband died in a car accident and she came back to Cork.

I focus on the rest of her story as well as I can. We're harried by the rain, by the shops' closing time— she has an errand to run on the way—and by people crowding on street corners waiting for buses that rarely appear. There's no time for me to figure out where we are, we're charging at great speed across a rough sea of umbrellas rattling at one another like fencing foils, her husband has reappeared in a law office in Los Angeles, I get a whiff of a wet dog, wet pants and a Chinese laundry as I zigzag, half a step behind her, having given up all hope of figuring out her story.

We get to the Tourist Office where, in a state of bewilderment, I wait my turn quietly. Things aren't moving fast enough for her liking, though, so she takes charge, wrangles with the woman at the information desk, makes a phone call and finally directs me to a house she stayed in once, not far from the centre, where a certain Mrs. Kennefik is already waiting for me. It's dark by now, and she orders me into a taxi with the address clearly marked on a slip of paper.

For a moment I consider inviting her to supper, but I don't even have time and, besides, there's no question of that, that's not what this is about. I sense that I haven't existed for her at all except as an opportunity for her to demonstrate her Christian charity. There's no place for desire, here; she expects nothing from me, we're not two individuals meeting each other, we have nothing to do with each other. It was simply a question of a wrong turning, and of an urgent need to avert the possibly catastrophic consequences of that wrong turning. Mission accomplished. Here I am again on the right track. I was going to lose my way and she's set me straight.

And what if I liked being lost?

No, no, that's not allowed. I picture her, finger to her mouth, alarm flickering in her eye. That's right out of the question. No, no, that's not allowed...

⇀

It's happened. I knew perfectly well that something would have to happen, and happen it did. In the small city of Cork, the cork popped. What a game I play with myself, what useless anguish. In the end everything takes its course, it always does. It has to. When I'm feeling confident, that's the way it goes. Knock and someone will let you in. And if they don't open up, knock, knock, and knock again. And see what opens up? This flower in the top of my head opens its great petals, and now I'm being propelled by the wind and lifting off gently, I'm taking wing, flying. I wheel around my room, watch myself sleeping, smiling, and leave neither by the window nor through the walls, but simply through the top of my head. I settle myself down on the tower and know I'm not dreaming. In the dark, strange city of Cork my room is a resting-place with a massive bed, heavy wallpaper, chandeliers. For hours I keep watch over my own tomb, laughing silently at being dead. I dream I'm not dreaming any more, everything is so unimportant now, pleasure, all that; the only things that matter to me are the things I've discovered in this sudden euphoria. There's no reality, that's what freedom is. Cork. The acrid smell of coal, narrow dark streets hemmed in with blind walls, a sense of the Middle Ages, smoke, damp heavy air, and it's my birthday and I'm alone and I have no one to talk to, but this is what I've wanted, this high dark room in this strange dark town.

Tonight I'm eating in a restaurant called Pizzaland, and Pizzaland obsesses me as the prototype of this neutral and antiseptic country the whole universe will turn into if the American empire succeeds in making its great dream of clean and inert uniformity come true. And these verses by an unknown poet keep running through my head:

> They are burning down all the flags
> In the garbage can behind McDonald's.

→

That was at the San Salvador bus stop in the bright and motley but oh so sad crowd. The Eagles' "Hotel California" was blaring from the loudspeakers, and the song had really nothing to do with anything when you left with I don't know how many grams of cocaine, climbing on board a bus called *La Inquietud*.

→

I'm obsessed with Pizzaland with its muted, boring Pizzalander clientele, and I'm drinking a third glass of red wine to my thirty-three years when I notice one completely drunk Pizzalander making faces at everyone, to the chagrin of the waitresses. "Bastards we are, bastards we stay!" A real wino, with a three-day beard and a coat too big for him, saying all the things no one dares say. Yes, this is the way it is in the Kingdom of Pizzaland: an asshole is an asshole and you don't need revolutionaries to teach you how to start a revolution. Everyone plays his role without envying the man next to him. The role of the drunken, fallen, abject, tearful and miserable wino, aggressively repeating that we are and will remain bastards, that he is and will always remain an asshole, that has to be one of the very best roles there is. And I myself in the role of the writer, that's a good character part for me, but in reality I'm a little boy crouching in a tree watching ants zigzag determinedly on the rough bark, and the only books I read are the adventures of Major Biggles by Captain W.E. Johns.

But one day someone told me you could change the world, and what I want now is to leave this imaginary kingdom. I want to get out of this restaurant, this antiseptic Irish pizzeria, get out of here with my Irish buddy, make faces at the middle classes, the fat cats and the Brits in the muddy streets of Cork. We're going to cross swords in freezing castles with sweating stone walls, full of secret rooms and nightmarish dungeons. Crows fly above the square tower, and the druids assembled in the woods pass their knowledge on to their descendants, and in the light I notice the brave Geoffroy and the valiant Lionheart who motion to me to join them in Valhalla.

→

Pleasure matters so very little... That's what I think again, sitting on the upper deck of a suburban bus whipped by the branches of trees that line this narrow road, hurtling towards Christmas on our cruel planet.

$\longrightarrow$

I'm still alone. Boredom tracks me down on the muddy little road linking Cork and Kinsale. No glory lightens the sky above me, just a greyish bank of clouds from which a nasty rain falls from time to time. Green Ireland... that's a poet's lousy symbol. Ireland is grey, black and brown, and existence isn't symbolic, it's dull and cold, wet and discouraging. I'm wearing all the clothes I could put on and am trying to keep my outstretched hand inside the spines of my umbrella as I hitchhike. I smile when a car comes close, and I swear at it when it passes me without stopping.

I'd have been better off staying in London with Jim and the others. The thought of what a great time they must be having in London bugs me more and more as my feet get wetter and wetter. But I don't want to have a good time. I've had enough of having a good time, getting drunk, getting stoned and dreaming of something else. That's why I left. I felt like a fattened chicken, plump and white, with tender flesh, steeped in beer and cognac, perfect for starving Third World people.

No, I don't want to have a good time any more. You poor fool, what do you think you're doing, at your age, standing at the side of the road waiting for God himself to put you in his chariot and drive you off to Paradise, up there somewhere, high, very high?

When I was little, Heaven was practically visible to the naked eye. But today, what with airplanes, satellites, rockets, radio-telescopes… So, theologian, what do you think now? About parallel worlds, levels of consciousness, anti-matter universes? Or that last incontrovertible limit, accessible here and now? You were born on earth, so stay on earth, that's what you've been wanting all along, probably, for an eternity.

Eternity? What's that? Cut those words out of your vocabulary. At this very moment there's nothing other than this road and this corner of Ireland, open your eyes.

And at this very moment a small truck stops, and I no longer doubt that I'm on the right road when its driver, a plumber by trade, father of four, here in this lost corner between two villages with unpronounceable names, starts talking almost at once about Madras, about Bombay, about the life he led over there when he was a sailor, and about the desire he often feels to leave again, his restlessness.

Yes, I want to go too, because there are two things I want to see, two things just for me: a corpse burning on a pyre, the nauseating smell of that, and a saint, someone who's achieved sainthood, a man like other men and different from them.

Afterwards I'll be able to tell the truth because I'll know what truth is, and I won't need to refer to what's acceptable and what's unacceptable, to standards of what's done and what's not done, to models of the left and of the right. And the indestructible hydra of identification of same with same and of like to known won't stand a chance any more against the indefinable dissolution of my atoms in the… But then there won't be the words any more to say what's what, and at that extreme I'll have stopped being the writer I don't wish to be, and the universe will take care of me because I'll be in the universe without differentiation, oh, yes! I will finally see the Great Whatever-It-Is face to face.

Trees and hedges and stones running with water slip by and past us. I'll be my own guru as I wait for a better one, as I wait to yield to the mirage. And this image itself emerging from inside of me, any faintly materialist thinker could explain that to me and relieve me of it, and I could respond that he, too… But now I need more and more urgently to find someone who has a better grasp of all this than I do, because all the guides I've met up to now have been useless, their knowledge petering out at exactly that point where it should have begun.

Trees and hedges and stones running with water. After a few kilometers I find myself at the edge of the road again with my thumb stuck out, my bag on my shoulder as there's no dry spot where I can put it down, my feet in the mud. I walk to a small nameless joint, a pub, an inn, drink a brown ale near a brazier, trying to stop shivering. Five burly labourers swallowing their bowls of soup and their mush cast their eyes in my direction from the corner, waiting for something to happen but nothing happens.

They'd be having a great time in London, this is the thought that runs through my mind. They'd be having a great time in Montreal, Quebec, San Francisco, Rio, Paris, Rome. In Laval, in Longueuil. Everywhere, in the Montreal Forum, in the bars on Saint-Denis Street, at the 321, in the Limelight, in the Shoeclack, everywhere, at this very minute, people are laughing, I can see them, I can hear them, and I'm here again, alone, on the edge of the road, my bag on my shoulder, my thumb stuck out.

Then later, near the end of the afternoon, I come to a quaint, touristy little village that's well thought out and organized, put together like a set in which only the extras are missing. And it's too bad, it's just too bad if I can no longer keep all this together. It isn't together at all, it has neither beginning nor end, it runs through my fingers like water, I push with all my might against my eyes, but what I see is nothing. I'm in limbo and everything is confused. I cry for Ireland through my tears, life is over there, and in this dream I can't hold the glass and drink from it, and my thirst troubles me perversely because it, too, is part of life.

→

Now I can say it. Now it has to be said, Angèle.
I'm dead. I've been dead for three years now; not
dead perhaps, but no longer living, that's for sure.
What's dead in me is... I can no longer imagine
anything, I can no longer see the signs or believe in
the angels that you hung on the walls all over our
apartment, in the stars on our clothes and in our hands
and in our eyes. That's all over now. It's nothing
serious, not very serious; it's even a little ridiculous,
and when I turn over these lost memories it's just a
pile of ashes. I can't help it, it all burned too brightly,
it burned me, you might say it purified me. But what
can be said with these learned words? What can be
known? Words have to enter into your very being
before you can really feel them. I don't talk to anyone
now, not ever. No more. Now I'm always alone with
myself, and I understand less and less of what happens.
I don't even know what I want beyond just wanting
to keep on the move. No one could ever explain me
to myself. I'm so afraid of intelligent people, of their
so beautiful ideas, their so beautiful books, their so
beautiful analyses, all that seems just laughable to me.
Pleasure makes me feel guilty, and unhappiness makes
me feel guilty and you, Angèle, who didn't feel guilty
for existing, what did you know that I didn't know?

$\longrightarrow$

So here I am in Kinsale with its postcard charm for tourists who want easy emotions. The place is deserted—it's off-season—and I make a bee-line for the first bar I see, a quiet bar where a scratchy old record plays old-fashioned airs. Nostalgia. Nostalgia and poetry and more: the kinds of things that could be revived and rekindled by the imagination. Give me two glasses of gin or two pints of Guinness, and I'll remember the bar where you sang leaning on the shoulder of the piano player who had a girl's name. I was sitting near the piano, and I was laughing because you loved me, because I was in love with the singer just like in the movies, only I hadn't foreseen the way it would end, though that was as obvious as in any bad script: the writer and the singer, crazy love, champagne, contractual obligations, domestic quarrels, jealous scenes, the broken music box, even that in keeping with everything one could imagine simple and pleasing to a middle-class audience carefully sheltered from reality; and whatever doesn't fit in nicely with the tragedy gets cut, the story has to be plain and uncomplicated, logical and psychological.

I finish my second beer, pay without saying a word, find a room and check out the village on foot. I visit a modest historical church, for I'm still taking my role seriously, even picking up the leaflets. It's still raining and I imagine the summer. Maybe it doesn't rain in the summer, maybe there's less mud in the streets, then, and more people in the bars; maybe the sad-looking sailboats in the little bay flutter in and out again gently as the sun sets between the islands that block the horizon.

After dinner I make one last attempt. I dress up properly and go into the best bar in the place. Nothing of any interest there, so I go back to my room and watch the colour television with the innkeeper's son in front of a coal fire, an old black-and-white American film, the life of a writer who slides into alcoholism, as all writers do because they have no right to do anything else, that's the way it is.

The actors deliver their lines at high speed as though trying to get rid of them before forgetting them, and they exaggerate every facial expression. The writer is pretty successful and starts drinking. At the first setback he begins drinking more heavily, becoming irritable, unbearable. Soon he has no more money, doesn't get out of bed any more, spends his days in bed, not writing any more, stuck, in debt, obsessed with booze, hiding the bottles, borrowing money. She is an angel straight from heaven. She loves him, tries to help him, but finally she can't take any more and abandons him. Then everything gets even worse for him, even darker, and he ends up killing himself.

So that's the story of writers, ravaged artists, booze and ruination. The innkeeper's son, who must be twenty-two years old, and who knows what life's all about, gets the message right away, understands the movie, sometimes even figures out in advance what's going to happen. But I don't understand a thing, I just want to get drunk as a skunk, and the bars are closed at this time, so I drink his goddamned tea just in order to drink, dreaming of drunkenness because I'm thirsty, and the longer the movie goes on the thirstier I get, and finally, instead of hitting the sack completely pissed and happy like a good writer, I spend the night with my eyes wide open listening to the goddamned bells of the goddamned historical church ringing every hour and every half-hour, waiting for day to break, thinking of you, always of you, and of sadness, of the great sadness of having lost you, for ever, for that at least I can count on for ever.

→

I finally fall asleep in the wee hours, and I dream. Every night now I'm dreaming, every night, and I'm anxious to get to bed and get into that state, over there, away from all constraints, into this marvellous imagination that I didn't think I had and that transports me, without my making the slightest effort, from surprise to surprise and from wonder to wonder. The dream, what has been said about the dream apart from trying to pretend that it didn't exist, that its only existence and only purpose was to mean something else, something other than it was, the reality, as if the dream wasn't itself real.

Tonight in my dream I am a racing cyclist, and though I haven't had any training at all, I participate in a big race and am just as good as the others. I have wings, I go very fast, I pump the pedals briskly, joyfully, with a brisk, joyful pain, I keep up with the pack. We're doing fine, we're doing great, we're just like a beer commercial on TV. I want to win, I want to win because I'm me, and even without training I can win because I'm me. When the others stop to rest for a bit, I work harder, I take the lead, I break away from them and lead the race. But just at the moment when I'm starting to get a bit tired, someone tells me the sprinters are arriving soon. The sprinters! I'd forgotten about them. I know I won't finish first, no way. I'm done in, and they've saved their energy for the last stretch. I'm angry, I wake up, I wake up, that's the best way of solving problems, and I end up fine waking up from life itself when I've really had enough of it. Awake! Wake up! And when I'm completely awake, how are you going to explain this dream to me in which you were one of those interpreters of dreams and you were expounding complicated theories without realizing that I'm the one who dreamed you?

→

I wake up, and surprisingly I'm in a very good mood. I feel at home everywhere now, this room I've slept in for one night might be the room I had when I was fifteen years old. Yes, that's it exactly. I'm never away from home and I have the impression of having known the people I meet for a long time. I spend a while with my head lolling on the pillow, considering the night's dreams. My good mood washes over me, cradles me like a wave.

It's Saturday, and the weather is superb. Huge blue sky, clear and sunny. I set off happy and confident after a substantial Irish breakfast: toast and coffee first, then eggs with bacon and sausages, porridge, more toast with jam. You come away feeling heavy and with your heart in your throat, and it takes till suppertime to digest it all, but it's included in the price of the room, so…

Not long afterwards, when I've got as far as a village called Bandon, I choose a small road leading to Killarney by way of Macroom. I've been told this is the best route, the most traveled. I regretfully forego the road to the sea, cross the village on foot and wait under the beautiful sun.

Five hours later, when I've walked ten or twelve kilometers, the sky is completely obscured, the rain has started pouring again, and I've been composing an insulting letter that I want to see appear in the Dublin newspapers addressed to the entire population of Ireland. There are few cars, and the rare imbeciles who pass me every quarter-hour are content either to stare at me as if I were some peculiar animal or to laugh stupidly while making a thumbs-down sign.

I start walking again with anger in my heart and fists clenched, mentally deleting a few sarcastic sentences in order to replace them with even nastier ones. I've reached the point of solving the Protestant-Catholic conflict by brilliantly demonstrating that Christian charity has disappeared from Ireland altogether. The Minister of Tourism is apologizing on behalf of the whole population ("We thank you so much, distinguished young foreigner") when I finally arrive at a kind of bar, a low, black stone roadside dwelling. Inside, two peasants are watching a boxing match on television, laughing uproariously every time one of the boxers takes a solid punch and grimaces in pain. I have the feeling I'm disturbing them. The uglier of the two leaves pretty quickly and the other refuses to chat. I drink a beer, eat what there is to eat, a chocolate bar and a bag of chips, and go on my way again convinced I've landed in a country of dolts. It starts raining seriously, the light fails, night falls, and I look like Tintin in The Black Island after the airplane crashed. So, Milou, we'll remember Ireland and the Irish.

I've given up hope when suddenly a car stops a few feet ahead of me. I walk up to it, expecting the whole time to see it move off again, a local pleasantry I've come to appreciate, but no. I open the car door, notice a rifle leaning against the front seat. But the driver, an elegant man of about fifty, simply moves the weapon to the back seat. It's a small calibre gun; he's on his way back from a pheasant shoot. I tell him my hitchhiking woes to comfort myself a little. He explains that people here are suspicious of strangers. I had figured that out. A few minutes later he drops me on the outskirts of Macroom. I should at least be able to sleep here; there should be a room in the village.

As I make my way to the centre, I stick my thumb out again just for the hell of it, and a car stops almost immediately, a blue Volkswagen filled with batteries, lengths of electrical wire, pliers, clips, screwdrivers, all kinds of tools, and the driver, a young electrician, talks to me finally the way you should talk to a visitor who's anxious to learn: about the IRA, the horrors being perpetrated daily in Northern Ireland about which the newspapers say nothing, the torture, vengeance, murders, atrocities suffered for centuries by the Irish people, driven back by the English to the bad lands of the West and South.

I've seen them, these areas, pink on my map, the Gaeltacht, "where the Irish are welcome," where they still speak the Irish language, that's where we are now. I get the sense that the batteries and wires and an electrician can come in handy when you want to make bombs, and O'Moriarty, that's his name, O'Moriarty, the Sailor, teaches me my first words of Irish before shaking my hand and taking leave of me in Killarney, as he can accompany me no longer. He has a rendezvous nearby, and I know well it's a secret rendezvous, a conspirators' night-time rendezvous, as I get out of his car in front of a Woolworth identical in every particular to those we had in Montreal not that long ago, with its big sign and gold lettering on a red background framed in gold.

I find a room for the night, leave my gear there and am ripe for one, two, three, four, as many pints of Guinness as I can manage in the little bar, hey, a cosy bar, full of young people, where I connect right away with John, Conn, Michael and the rest, and with Ray, a mining engineer just back from Canada, who, before I get too pissed, explains the process of extracting oil from bituminous sands and some other process that has something to do with someone called

Renée Savard whom he met in a bar in the old part of
Quebec City, and finally I'm pissed and they're pissed
and the evening is off to a great start in a familiar fug,
smoke, semi-darkness, a mass of human warmth,
understanding smiles, floods of beer, winks, but at
eleven o'clock, yes, eleven o'clock on the dot, the
lights brighten harshly and it's all over. It reminds
me of the Bouvillon, when they'd send us packing at
three in the morning, and we'd hang back while they
vacuumed the floor after piling the chairs on the
tables, all except for our table where we were nursing
the last beers that we'd ordered in bulk at last call
and that we now clung to desperately. Here, though,
no one protests, and without much lingering the place
empties. At eleven o'clock on a Saturday night, it's
over. We find ourselves outside and head for a
discotheque that's still open, but there's a crowd at
the door. We're all lined up outside in an unpleasant
drizzle, and in the end my heart isn't in it any more,
or maybe I'm too pissed. Anyway, the magic's gone
and I call it a night.

→

It rains again on Sunday. I've drunk a great deal, and take advantage of the day to settle my stomach. My bowels are in an uproar, a kind of salty taste of rendered fat twists through my sick intestines. A lost Sunday. I'm worthless, I want nothing, am just waiting for it to be over. I'm walking in a sort of garden, half park, half wood, memories are coming back to me, a stream of fuzzy memories invading my mind, a series of more or less precise images, fleeting little scenes, drifting, sheer confusion of memory, a sudden accumulation around one name, then some other thing, vague associations without edge or strength, without details, without ever going so far as to be precise, without moments, sensations, reality, words, a simple mixture, very close to death, of inexistence, through neglect, through lack of interest, heavy, grey, oily waves, tragic haziness of aborted states of mind. The rain is falling on a big grey lake surrounded by damp, rich lawns, veils of fog caught on bare trees. I am floating painfully, suspended in a great quantity of water that sometimes falls in a vaporized drizzle and soaks me through. I have drowned somewhere, and from the bottom of the lake I'm contemplating the rain that's weighing everything down until tomorrow.

—➤

Hitchhiking. I've had enough of its chanciness, enough of its glories. Abandoned by a young land-surveyor in a commercial centre in suburban Limerick, I watch in complete disgust while the cars stream past me, as hermetically sealed as cans of sardines. Families crammed in with bags of groceries, people who've gone to the corner of the street for a pack of cigarettes. Feet wet, soaked, drenched with water like a sponge, drenched with the countryside, grass, old churches, stone walls, hedges, trees in the rain, muddy villages, the hissing of tires, I have only one idea in my head: the train. So much for heroism. The train to Dublin.

⟶

I notice her right away on the station platform with her shawls, her long coloured skirts, her bright red hair, her old-fashioned high-heeled button boots. An artist, an actress, a madwoman, someone to talk to.

Ah! Climbing aboard a train, clambering up the steps, hoisting yourself up to the carriage, feeling the weight of your baggage on your shoulder, finding yourself wedged into the narrow corridor that turns a sharp corner. Seated in fine, comfortable armchairs, my future traveling companions flash glances over the top of their newspapers at the new arrival who's come to disturb their peace. I pass quickly through two railway cars, discovering her settling into her seat. Always the gentleman, I help her put her bag on the luggage rack while checking out her waist which curves in under her fitted blouse, her round arms, her slightly dimpled hands. "May I sit here?" I play with my halting English, I do the young foreigner off-season on Irish roads bit. Sure, it's romantic, and from her manner of smiling I know full well that...

At once, or almost at once, the train sets off again. We're on our way in the warm under the changing sky, white and grey clouds, the sun putting in an appearance, disappearing, and another storm, then more sun. We drink a delicious beer and I hope that the trip will last a long time, forever. I could chat all the way to India. Ensconced on either side of the little folding table that we've set up between our seats, we look at each other, we laugh, we talk as though we'd been reunited at long last. An unusual girl. Finally I've touched down, here I am finally in the real Ireland, no longer in the Ireland of pheasant hunters, boxing enthusiasts, mud-carriers, dumb students, mean farmers, petty businessmen. Finally I'm in the Ireland of artists, the Ireland of Joyce, Synge, Behan, Beckett, Yeats and Swift, and I can talk. Finally I'm no longer this ranter, this poor idiot, this weird foreigner. A door is opening, she is opening it for me, and beyond is an Ireland I recognize.

We understand each other immediately. Immediately we're alone in the world, and our neighbours are watching us disapprovingly. We're laughing too much, we're talking too much, and our eyes are shining too much with desire. The countryside slips past in the noise of the wheels and the rails, nicely framed by the rectangle of the window. We have lots to say to each other, making words is like a deliverance after such a long transatlantic absence, we give each other the works, we do her Irish Catholic and my Quebec Catholic in Jesus Christ our Lord, on the velvet seats on each side of the table where we pile up the beers and the golden words that pour out and make us tremble and live in the teasing desire to touch each other already in these first minutes of our perpetual adoration of a life that's finally writ large because we both believe in beauty.

$\longrightarrow$

Dublin. We buy a newspaper, she helps me find a room for the night, and then I take her to the theatre where she's playing her first part. I'll see her again tomorrow evening. We part with a quick kiss and lots of promises in our eyes. I spend the night in a strange room on a deserted floor of an old house. The whole family has moved into the basement, something to do with saving on the winter heating bills. The room is glacial but there's a radiator run by a coin-operated meter.

The next day I tour the city under its great grey sky, crossing the bridges over the oily Liffey. Where am I? Grey, gloomy, heavy, and joyless, the Irish come and go in their daily lives. On street-corners angelic choirs sing Christmas carols to collect money for all kinds of good causes, the Red Cross, sick children, paraplegics, cancer, multiple sclerosis, the poor, the ugly and the wretched. The latest Pink Floyd plays in all the music stores, hammering out revolt in every line. We don't need no education. The sadness of Dublin, a poor little nordic city crushed by the splendour of its esplanades and its monuments. This is how I imagine Leningrad, or Vladivostok.

Under these lugubrious skies, the stink of famine and potatoes lurks amidst the smell of coal. People make the sign of the cross as they pass the churches. You could imagine yourself in the Quebec of 1954.

In all this grey you see only the eyes, blue and light, green and watery, the hair, blond, red, pale and bright at the same time, and a sort of overwhelming fatalism like an accumulation of grief crying and raining and languishing the length of streets buffeted by the grey wind. I lunch with a young couple from Northern Ireland who reluctantly tell me about the climate of suspicion that reigns there, the continual searches in stores, on the street, and assure me that it all seems much worse in the newspapers than it is in reality, that life is about as quiet as elsewhere and it's just the atmosphere of fear and foreboding that gets in the way of a normal existence. At dinner I find myself next to a retired British import-export businessman who tells me about the fundamental changes Dublin has undergone over the past fifteen years, about the much slower, provincial life people used to lead there. Slower? What must it have been like? Already I feel as though I'm traveling in the past.

An evening of theatre, the play entitled "Once a Catholic..." and it begins with the Tantum ergo. I'm flooded with high school memories, the compulsory Friday mass, the navy blue blazer with the crest, the grey pants, the burgundy-coloured tie, the smell of incense and the freedom that followed in the chaos of our running for our schoolbags stuffed with books and exercise books, clean, elitist little students storming the buses with our shouts and our tricks, our squabbles and our smug little universe.

Here, the action takes place in a convent, and the heroine is torn between an outing organized by the sisters in Fatima and the illicit pleasures of rock 'n roll. I recognize the morbid climate that produced me, the anguish of confessing the appeal of the flesh, masturbation, the first sinful touching, the obsession with breasts and other parts of the body glimpsed in our dictionaries, disguised as works of art, satyrs carrying nymphs in their strong arms, their muscled thighs always hiding their sex. Terrified as I was of any possible abnormality, I would wonder if their sex looked like mine.

Kate only has one line, and her line only has one word. She says "Present" when her name is called. After the play I strut my stuff with her. That's the best way of beginning a career, present, I'm here, here I am, here and now, stage presence is the most important quality in an actor or actress, and on top of that it's a character part as she plays the Polish student and has just the one word to express that, rolling her "r" like a foreigner trying not to reveal her origins and not succeeding, in spite of herself, in hiding an inexpressible and undeniable Slavic charm.

All that in a single word, Kate, that's marvelous, and I assure her that I found her marvelous. I lay it on thick, I who, in the wings, in Montreal, when I'd go looking for Angèle, would skulk in a corner, incapable of saying a word.

It's eleven o'clock when we leave the theatre, and the pubs are already closed; we visit her friend Barbra, a sweet, sad student who's listening to Dylan, Van Morrison and Gérard Lenorman, pining for her Moroccan lover. The two of them have already adopted me, want to turn me into a real Irishman. We talk quietly at the corner of the coal fireplace, banal sentences, unimportant details, bland exchanges, stages to get through as you never begin without any preamble, you dawdle in the past and then the present and the future, but I know well that eternity is here somewhere over our heads and always readily available, at that very moment, for example, when we kiss at the corner of a park at 3:30 in the morning in a kind of soft moist air softened further by birdsong, and I with one hand in her hair and the other around her waist, I keep my eyes open, I see the rows of houses with Georgian doors, I see the clear sky tinged with blue, a few pale grey clouds floating at the break of dawn, I listen, I feel, I hear and I wonder what she is surrendering herself to as she surrenders herself against me like this, what is this old romantic dream that's here, in my arms, a dream that I hold close to me, then my tongue is in her mouth and I watch these closed eyes, this gift that gives me nothing, our tongues going round and round each other's mouths with the saliva mixing, the soft skin enveloping the engorged flesh of the lips we press against each other, watch our two bodies that cling to each other and that will never blend into each other, what am I doing here? What are we doing here? The seconds pass, become minutes. It happens too often to me now that I don't understand anything about these desires to couple, these passing lovers I watch without envy. What are you doing? What do you think you've found? And I try to take my tongue back without upsetting her, to put an end to this kiss that's leading nowhere and should stop, that really should stop sooner or later.

We part. I know she's dying to invite me to spend what's left of the night at her place, and that she doesn't dare, the stages, the fear of seeming too easy, better to wait a bit, I'll see her again tomorrow, she's inviting me for high tea, and softly I head back to my place and I sleep in the peace and certainty known by all those for whom a great and reassuring love awaits.

→

Rain, rain, rain, interminable rain. Hours and minutes with thousands of words piling up, hours and fractions of seconds across time, across space and its tiny expanses, eating, putting food in your mouth, chewing, swallowing, then getting up, walking, waiting at crossroads, finding another street, all these trivial details that amount to a life when you're there without knowing why you're there, a pathetic creature with no known destination drifting slowly, incapable of anything else.

I visit the museum, mostly the Irish rooms, this long history of struggle, wretchedness, rebuff; so many things to learn from prehistoric times and this old Celtic foundation with its extraordinary language, its towns with curious names like Emain, Tara, Dinn Rigg, Temuir Erann, Cruachain, its law, its code, its strange monarchy, then an endless succession of invasions, and always the same background of appalling misery, famine after famine, cholera, poverty, economic subjugation, political domination, the interminable fight for independence, to safeguard something. Safeguard what? Religious wars grafted onto economic liberation, the English Protestant minority dominating an entire people, all these unknown names—it would take a lifetime to become Irish, to have this past, this history, this culture inscribed in one's veins, genes, chromosomes, memory.

So many things to learn. Two million dead between 1846 and 1851. Two million human lives, individual destinies, sufferings, with days and days without bread, perhaps occasionally a meagre meal, perhaps loves, laughter, anger, sexual fantasies, small hopes, desires, joys we will never know because that's all there is, two million dead. They rate no more than a mention in the history books, and then there's the handful of heroes who may have just been fools.

Fortunately there is the Trinity College library with its indisputable solace, its well-worn volumes with copper and gold reflections, a timeless refuge to engage in bookish toil with the patience of an ant under the reassuring eyes of the white marble busts of all human sages. And then, too, for moments of discouragement, there are these romantic pubs where Joyce and Yeats and Synge and O'Casey, Beckett, Oscar Wilde and Shaw carved their names with a knife before going on their way, fleeing this too-small world.

I arrive at Kate's in time for high tea, brimming with my recently acquired learning, and we talk, talk, talk, interweaving politics, art and religion.

⇢

We're forever colonized culturally, you know. In Quebec as in Ireland, in England as in the United States. Culture is when others take over, when others take us over to make us what they are, when they give us their words to see and feel and think and speak, and it matters little whether the words be English, French or Chinese, feminine, masculine or neuter. They're never neutral. Words are never neutral, they deform everything, they run us out of the marvelous countries of childhood, they circumscribe us, limit us and constrain us, and when we enter into a language we have no idea what we're getting into. It's a religion, it's a cathedral, it's a house, it's a garment and, try as we might, we fight that language in vain, we're done for. Purity is no longer possible, our view narrows, our eyes dull. Slowly we grow blind, and we should be doing our utmost to learn to see again, but between us and what we really are stands a barrier of thousands of words with their own history, their connotations, their associations, their dust, their past, their deformations, their woe. And the only escape for me right now is flight, an accelerated flight from what always catches up with me, that catches up with me quickly, that lands on me and prevents me from seeing, that blocks my mouth, blocks my freedom. I don't want to go blind. There is no one in the world can give me my freedom, not even the most great and the most free, because the word great and the word free are still words. I abhor words, you know. Yes, I am a writer and I abhor all the words that haunt me and harass me and persecute me, and the word writer is one of those because what do you think it is, to be a writer? Am I a writer when I speak? When I take a bus? Am I a writer in the bathtub? When I'm eating? And you who take me for a writer, what do you think I am, a word?

The universe is within me, and that's what I can't find. The universe is outside of me, too, and I am neither outside nor inside but elsewhere, in the indeterminate zone of human fiction. We're living in fiction. Did you know that? We're not ourselves, we see nothing, we feel nothing of what's happening, even of what's happening at this very instant, this precise moment, we're just component parts of a code, a vast social, political, economic, cultural code, this dog's dinner, this splodge of laughter and completely interchangeable feelings that comes closer and closer to exploding without ever actually getting to that point, because the word revolution is never the actual revolution. I'm signalling to you, Kate, with small signs that signify, though it's nonsense. I would like you to understand this. I even think paradoxically that you might be able to understand it. I hope you will manage to understand, but what the hell... I find even that discouraging. I'd like to talk to the birds, to the Dublin pigeons, to the trees in St. Stephen's Green, to the land of Ireland that we call Irish and that isn't Irish. Imagine a shovelful of Irish earth transported to London. Imagine Ireland transported shovel by shovel and becoming the earth of England, the very same earth. I'd like to talk to the worms, to the worms tunneling their way through this earth, which isn't even "dirt" or "clay" or "wet," but simply that which rubs against us, fills our eyes, feeds us, lives with us, lengthens us, penetrates us, receives us, so that there's no more difference between the universe and ourselves, no more separation, no more break... Mad, yes, and yet who can boast of knowing more about it all than I do? Who knows the answer to the question that has no answer? People have agreed to die in the narrow confines of their fictional roles: plumber, lawyer, head of a family, broken-hearted lover, whatever it may be. It would have been possible for me to be a writer, too, till the end of my days, but I refuse. I refuse. I accept this sad predicament that prevents me from being man and god at one and the same time. I don't understand this determination to defend a culture as though salvation were to be found there. Québécois. Irish. Sure, it's been known to happen. I've been known to allow myself to admire people who set great store by that very cause, who defended it to the death. And then? Where do nations stop, where can borders be drawn? Empires, countries, provinces, regions, villages, all the way to solitude. We can divide ad infinitum. Groups, sub-groups, sub-sub-groups. Types, species, families, individuals. None of it's of any further interest to me. I aspire to eternity, that's what I want. I know it exists and I know where it is for that instant when I'm talking to you. Further, higher, lower, nearer, what does it matter? The word eternal is an invention that diverts us from eternity. Eternity is in what comes into me and goes out of me too quickly for me to grasp. Mad, yes. You know as well as I do, the whole world is going mad. Writers, artists, scientists are going mad, and those who aren't going mad stay the way they are, ordinary people happy to run to the human garbage-heap without ever shivering with horror and without having known ecstasy, ordinary folks who die without ever being really dead, people who disappear without leaving any trace. Sometimes I envy them for living in this universe full of meaning, money the measure of everything, politics at every turn, unthinking sex, rest and relaxation. Eternity is beyond all measure. How could we talk about eternity? Poetry is not given to everyone. First we have to take possession of silence and silence the voice of everything in us that is not of us. Words are too much. We talk too much, we read too much, and we write too much. We give meaning to what should not be more than sound. The people of the East are right: mantras and silence.

→

Kate listens to me and I know I am seducing her. We're both watching the flames in the hearth, drinking red wine, and from time to time my gaze meets hers and I see her eyes shining. I know perfectly well what's going on. Something in her is becoming soft and warm. It's so easy to seduce. I seduce myself, I seduce myself and I disgust myself. I let the wine speak through me, and am carried away by its eloquence. Outside it's still raining and we're been here for hours. Darkness has engulfed the room. Kate lights a little lamp and moves close to me. Any minute now I'll take her in my arms and kiss her. Perhaps we will tell each other sweet nothings. We will undress each other, button by button, one sleeve after the other, clinging to each other in our stockinged feet, stumbling out of our jeans, discovering small areas of flesh we'll caress gently. I can easily imagine the whole scene, I've lived it so many times already and I'm in no hurry. I'd much rather talk, empty my brain. She is young, Kate, not much more than twenty years old. For her, this will still be new, maybe magical. A dream. Later she'll be angry with herself, perhaps; she'll tell herself that she's been had. But what can I do? She likes me, she wants it. It's in vain that I tell her the worst things about myself, warn her that I'm just a traveler, blacken myself as much as I can, drink like a drunk. Destiny is pushing us together and we can't avoid it. I would have to have the strength to get up and leave, and I'm not capable of that. I'm too fond of feeling good, staying on, talking, laughing. I've suffered enough, I tell her, to not want to suffer any more. That doesn't do any good. I rarely let myself get too bothered. I'm no Prince Charming, you know, just another ordinary Joe who hasn't lived up to his dreams. Life, its easiness, its trivialities. And at that moment I feel keenly everything that I lack, all the energy and enthusiasm needed for poetry, needed for this moment to take off and ignite.

I've said too much, too much about discouragement, about despair. She wants, she no longer wants, she knows now that it will lead nowhere, but there's something else in her, a wish, perhaps, to comfort a disappointed little boy who knows too much and can no longer have any fun. I know that I know that I know that I...

In spite of it all we end up stretching out on the narrow bed, in spite of everything my sex hardens along her body and I slowly relax. At that point questions have a way of vanishing. Mystery takes the upper hand. There's something holy in even the most banal of loves, the most ill-matched couples, the briefest liaisons. Instinct upsets everything. The swelling of the penis puts an end to the interior monologue. Sometimes a few moments of misgiving filter through, a few moments of appreciation, of commentary, but in between these moments, nothing, a perfect void, a kind of nirvana. The satisfaction of getting the job done, of responding to the needs of the species. I hold her in my arms and an unexpected happiness suffuses my whole being. Finally naked, we cling to each other, little lovers lost in a nameless room lit by the single flame in the hearth, shivering with cold and with pleasure in each other's arms. Then under the covers, for a long time I caress Kate's soft white skin without succeeding in calming her timid and tense adolescent nervousness, so very tense that she will not let me enter her.

$$\longrightarrow$$

I move in with Kate. I can stay with her as long as I like, she says, and of course that makes me wish to be on my way at once. In an instant I picture myself ending my days in Dublin, becoming an Irish citizen, starting over with a life just like the old one, with a sense of having gone back in time twenty years, and a foreign language slowly erasing my memory of what I would have been. We visit our friends and cheer them up, we have our projects and our dreams, our worries and our joys, our sorrows and our moments of confusion, and all I have to do is wait for the pubs to open and dream that I will go on my way one day since I will never have gone on my way.

Rain, rain, rain, the next day as well, all the details, the price of rooms, Irish names, the pubs closing at eleven o'clock, the coal fires, twenty-six dollars a week, the toilets down the hall, the hotel near the bookstore across from the park, the little lock on the canal, the black hookers on the street corner, the chic boutiques near the university, the too wide esplanade and all the shops bursting with Christmas shoppers, the French waitress at Pizzaland I prefer to speak to in English because she doesn't understand my Québécois accent, all this enters into me and flows inside me and gets mixed up in my mind.

I've drunk too much, I'm ill, diarrhea and vomiting, I'm emptying myself out of both ends, I spend the day in bed, reading, listening to the radio, waiting for Kate to get back, motherly with syrup and a bag of groceries, and I entertain myself by making her laugh, waiting, waiting, waiting to go on my way. I'm sick. I'm fine. I don't give a damn. I have the runs. I'm throwing up every fifteen minutes. I rush to the freezing toilet where December's cold north wind gusts in through the unsealed frame of the badly fitting window, and I kneel before the bowl and writhe as I rid myself of my lies. I observe the cold porcelain and the yellow stains on the rim coldly, and it doesn't matter. It's as though even my suffering were a foreigner. I despise the wretched soul she's visiting. Then, feverish and drenched in sweat, I hurry back to lie down under as many blankets as I could find, and I shiver from head to toe. Kate looks after me, and I give myself up to her like a child. I never again want to have to decide anything for myself. I leave everything to her and to Providence, and I still haven't succeeded in loving. I feel only emptiness, an unsettling and bitter emptiness.

At the end of the day the crisis is past, and I sit quietly in front of the fireplace listening on French radio to demented rock 'n roll broadcasts with a frantic disk jockey shouting who knows what over the music of old 45s.

The next day my head is still heavy. Kate brings me a Celtic remedy that looks like a mixture of white paint, cold syrup and ether, concocted by an old pharmaceutical druid. Then we go around the book shops—yet more books that'll keep me clear of the real life I'd like to lead if I could only succeed in disconnecting from this deformed old brain stuffed with scraps of paper and scribblings.

In a copy of a Book of Nonsense opened at random I find the limerick section. Limerick is where I met Kate, and in this section the book falls open at a limerick of Kipling's entitled Quebec. Is this a sign? And what does it signify?

I don't understand a word of it, and as I believe not in signs but in material, observable, measurable and empirical reality, I'm quite content that it all be nonsense.

There's a party in the evening. Kate's happy; it's the last night of the play, friends have come from Cork, and perhaps I'll spend the Christmas holidays here. All these tiny apartments and the people all seeming like conspirators, life is so gloomy, everyone seeking light in their own way, like Conor, who throws himself at everyone, brimming over with love. He finally knocks me down, bites me on the neck and grabs my nuts shouting "Balls, balls, balls." I'm too drunk to get up, and all three of us end up on the floor, him and me and Kate, with Kate trying to help me up, and isn't it grand, my Irish friends, that something is finally happening.

Kate is happy. Barbra says to me, "Have you ever seen her with such a smile?" I certainly have not. How could I have? I didn't know her before. But was I brought into the world to settle down and make an Irishwoman happy?

We've bet on the horses and haven't won a penny. We've drunk hot whiskeys at Toner's on Baggot Street. We've seen the pink and green seafront houses in Dun Laoghaire like two romantic lovers. When I'm happy I always talk a lot. Angèle often used to sing me the Dalida song, "You were as happy as an Italian when he knows he'll have love and wine." And I remember Pamela who appreciated my mystical ravings "mainly when you are high on wine." High on wine is easy. But sober? True mysticism begins when you sober up.

Yes, I knew, I already knew how to have a good time, but now I've changed my mind, now I know there's something else tugging me forward, something I'll never reach, because I don't even want to reach it, because if I were to reach it I'd flee in the opposite direction. Of course it happened like that and it didn't happen at all like that. Within every second there's an entire novel, with a beginning and an end, with all its interweaving of causes and effects and its infinite horizontal and vertical dimensions. But what I'm left with now is this, hardly a trace, the tender scent of a body of a certain size, the heaviness of that amount of flesh and the particular softness of the skin, fine blonde hair that I stroked on her shoulder, the impression that I understood everything about people like me, people seeking the light, and the impression, too, that I cannot transmit this light because I don't have it in me, neither light nor peace nor love, and this split, this something in the depths that's broken, like a painful death made up of a thousand little details, my very own death, the one I must pass through, will pass through, drinking to the end, to the lees. I didn't know how to love, I've never known how to love, someone should teach me, forcing it down my throat, look at your misery, your despair, feel it, inhale it, do you understand why you're suffering? Take another look, suffocate some more, still more, you've never loved anything but that, yourself, a mirage.

This evening Kate is leaving for a last meeting and I say goodbye to her, goodbye, we kiss, goodbye Kate, we will never see each other again, when she gets back I'll have gone, but you can stay, if you want, if you change your mind, the ferry didn't sail yesterday, the sea was too high, and after all it's nearly Christmas, we could spend it together, goodbye Kate, it was nice, it was good to be here, too good, I was going to become Irish but I can't, I still have far to go, I must go, I must leave where it's good and go to where I cannot live, to where I should die, die in order to become other than I am.

And alone, but not yet really alone, I cook myself some Brussels sprouts in the kitchenette that's as cold as a fridge, and I drink some Vichy water, and I collect my things and I stuff them into my bag one more time, and one more time I swing my bag on to my shoulder, and I open the door for the last time and for the last time hide the key in its hiding place, and I walk to the docks one more time and one more time I make the ferry crossing, crossing appearances, crossing fear, crossing death, crossing the Irish Sea.

Going on my way, that's the only time I'm fine, when the mooring lines are rewound on the gigantic winches, when the dock slowly recedes, and the sea again surrounds the great metal ship, the prow turning towards the open sea, testing, hesitant, slapped by the first waves, when there's nothing more ahead than the black night and the heavy black water, when the lights of the coast fade into the distance and we gather speed and begin to glide and dance and skip over the waves. When image follows image without ever solidifying, and we glide with them, fluid and mobile, when it's all ephemeral and insubstantial and unattainable. When you know this moment will never happen again, that this too will pass, will pass without your ever having been able to grasp it. And it's as though I was seeing myself from the boat, standing on the dock. It's as though I was seeing myself from the dock, standing on the boat. It's as though I were able to say goodbye to myself and carry on two lives that would never meet up again. After four days in Kate's bed I'm leaving Ireland, watching from the aft bridge as the lights flicker, as the lights of the buoys and the lighthouse fade and then flare again, with this impenetrable and deep sense of a moment of no return, gliding through time that's fluid and no longer cut by the abrupt ticking of the second hand, time freed from constraints and pouring in a single movement, a single flux, carrying all at once the boat, and the black sea, and the red and green of the lighthouse, and the expanse of the sky, and myself leaning over the railing as in the best romantic fiction.

fin

About the Author

In 1967 Louis Gauthier published his first novel, *Anna,* when he was only 21 years old. This was followed by the publication of *Les Aventures de Sivis Pacem et Para Bellum (Tome I)* in 1969 and *Les grands légumes célestes vous parlent* in 1973. In 1978 his novel *Souvenir du San Chiquita* came out, but he did not publish again for another six years, when *Voyage en Irlande avec un parapluie* came out, followed by *Le Pont de Londres* four years later.

Louis Gauthier lives in Montreal, where he earns his living primarily in the fields of editing and advertising. He was the president of the Quebec Writers' Union (UNEQ) in 1997 and 1998. He continues to travel.

ABOUT THE TRANSLATOR

Linda Leith is the author of two novels, *Birds of Passage* and *The Tragedy Queen*. Publisher and editor of *Matrix* magazine for six years, she is editor of the anthology *Telling Differences: New English Fiction from Quebec*, and the author of *Introducing Hugh MacLennan's Two Solitudes*. She was born in Northern Ireland and lives in Montreal.

Printed in October 1999 by

ON DEMAND PRINTING INC.

in Longueuil, Quebec